PINKY and REX
and the
Perfect Pumpkin

PINKY and REX
and the
Perfect Pumpkin

by James Howe
illustrated by Melissa Sweet

SCHOLASTIC INC.
New York Toronto London Auckland Sydney
Mexico City New Delhi Hong Kong

Author's Note

I am grateful to my daughter, Zoey Howe, and my niece, Rachel Imershein, for giving me the title and two handwritten pages of their own first draft of *Pinky and Rex and the Perfect Pumpkin*. While the story in this book is my invention, the pumpkin-picking weekend is a family tradition which Zoey and Rachel very much wanted me to write about. They came up with the idea when they were both in the third grade. At the time of publication, they are in the sixth grade. All the while, they managed to keep the whole thing a secret from their grandparents! This book is their gift to Grandma Lois and Grandpa Charles Imershein.

I want to acknowledge, too, my niece and Rachel's younger sister, Jordana, who is a vital part of the pumpkin-picking tradition. My love to them all.

•

ISBN 0-439-13340-8

12 11 10 9 8 7 6 5 4 3 2 1   9/9 0 1 2/0 3 4/0

Printed in the U.S.A.   23

First Scholastic printing, October 1998

To Grandma Lois and Grandpa Charles, and their pumpkin pickers—Zoey, Rachel, and Jordana
—J. H.

To Julia
—M. S.

Contents

Chapter 1

Abby

"They're here!" Rex shouted from the front yard. "Pinky! Amanda! Your grandparents are here!"

Pinky and Amanda burst out of their house, the screen door slamming shut behind them.

"Whoa!" their grandfather laughed, as Amanda wrapped herself around his

legs. "At least let me get out of the car, Amanda-panda!"

"You *are* out of the car, Grandpa!" Amanda cried. "And, anyway, I thought you would never get here!"

"Would Grandma and I miss pumpkin-picking weekend?"

"Hi, Grandpa!" Pinky called out.

"Hi, Pinky! And there's Rex! How's my good-as-a-granddaughter?"

"Great!" Rex answered. She loved it when Pinky's grandfather called her his good-as-a-granddaughter. Rex was Pinky's across-the-street neighbor—*and* his best friend in the whole world—but as far as Pinky's grandparents were concerned, she was one of the family.

"So, Rex," Grandma asked, "are you all set to go pumpkin picking?"

"I've been packed for a week!" Rex replied.

"Better put your bag in the car, then," Grandpa said. "As soon as Abby gets here, we'll be on our way!"

Abby was Pinky and Amanda's cousin. She lived a couple of hours away and always joined them for pumpkin picking at their grandparents' weekend house at the lake. Rex liked Abby. She and Abby and Pinky were all the same age and enjoyed doing many of the same things.

On past pumpkin-picking weekends, there had been problems sometimes when Pinky's little sister Amanda had been left out. Rex remembered what her parents had said to her that morning: "Try extra hard to include Amanda this year." Rex made a silent promise to herself that she would try.

"Are we going to stop at the Red Rooster for lunch?" she heard Amanda ask.

"Of course," Grandma answered as a car pulled into the driveway. "It's part of our tradition, isn't it?"

The car came to a stop, and out jumped Abby. "Pinky! Amanda!" Abby shouted, as she ran past Rex to hug her cousins.

"Hi, Abby!" Rex called out, but Abby didn't seem to hear her.

"Abby, hi!" she called again. Abby didn't even turn her head.

Rex's parents had come from their house across the street to join the other grown-ups who were gathering in the yard. Everyone was talking about what a fun weekend the children were going to have. Rex was no longer sure how much fun it was going to be.

Chapter 2
The Perfect Day

All the way in the car, Grandma and Grandpa kept saying how perfect the day was. The perfect day for looking for the perfect pumpkin. The perfect start of a perfect weekend. Rex gazed out the window at the clear blue sky and the trees with their many-colored leaves and thought, *I want to go home.*

Everything felt different. Wrong, somehow. It wasn't Grandma and Grandpa. They were the same as always. They asked Rex how her summer had been and how she liked her new teacher. They even remembered what she would order at the Red Rooster: a hot dog with nothing on it, a large order of french fries, and a vanilla milk shake.

No, it wasn't Grandma and Grandpa.

It was Abby. And Amanda. And Pinky.

The three cousins buzzed and whispered and laughed among themselves. They started practically every sentence with "Remember the time we . . ." or "Let's do *this* this weekend . . ." or "Let's do *that* this weekend . . ." And every time Rex tried to join the conversation, Abby cut her off.

"Here it is!" Pinky shouted, not long after they had left the Red Rooster.

"Meadowbrook Farm!" Amanda called out.

"Home of the perfect pumpkins!" Abby cried.

Rex said not a word.

"Do you feel all right, Rex?" Grandma asked softly as they were getting out of the car. "You've been so quiet."

"I'm okay," Rex muttered.

Grandpa put his hand on her shoulder.

"Then what do you say we do some serious pumpkin picking?"

Rex smiled. "Okay," she said.

But just as she started to feel better, Grandpa said to his wife, "Isn't it nice to see how well the cousins are getting along this year?"

"I'll say," Grandma replied. "For once, Amanda isn't being left out."

Rex bit her lip to keep from crying.

Chapter 3

Pumpkin Picking

On the hay wagon, Grandma reminded everyone of the rules. "You can pick one pumpkin each to take home to carve with your parents," she said. "Any pumpkin at all. No matter how big."

"No matter how small," the kids chanted.

The familiar sound of the words began to cheer Rex up.

"What about gourds?" Amanda asked.

"As many gourds as you want. But the four of you have to find the perfect pumpkin together. That's the pumpkin we'll carve tonight."

"Last stop!" the driver called out as the wagon came to a halt in the middle of a huge field filled with pumpkins. "Have fun!"

"Wow!" Rex said, jumping down from

the wagon. "Do you know what I'd call this place?"

"What?" Pinky asked.

"The Pumpkin Ocean!" said Rex.

Everybody laughed—everybody but Abby.

"Pinky! Amanda!" Abby called out. "Follow me. The best pumpkins are over here."

Rex ran after the others to keep up.

There were so many pumpkins that it was easy to find the ones to take home. Agreeing on the perfect pumpkin, however, was much, much harder.

As each pumpkin was suggested, someone was sure to say, "Too small!" or "Too skinny!" or "That one's got a bad spot!"

When it was Rex doing the suggesting, she noticed that Abby would not only find something wrong with the pumpkin, she would roll her eyes or snicker or whisper in Pinky's ear. One time, she even said, "That's the stupidest-looking pumpkin I ever saw. Isn't it, Pinky?"

Pinky didn't answer. He only glanced at Rex, and when his eyes met hers, his cheeks turned bright red.

Chapter 4

Goofus

"It took you a long time," Grandpa exclaimed that night after dinner, "but you surely did find the perfect pumpkin!"

The pumpkin sat in the center of the dining-room table, just waiting to be carved. Grandma was in the kitchen making hot chocolate, which they would have with the donuts they had bought at the farm. Everything was going the way it was supposed to go, at last. Rex wondered if she had only imagined that things were different.

"Hot chocolate and donuts!" Grandma called out.

"Let the carving begin!" Grandpa declared.

As everyone gathered around the table, Amanda asked, "How come we do the same things the same way every year?"

"Because it's tradition," said Pinky.

"So what?" Amanda asked.

"Traditions give you something to look forward to," Rex said.

"Exactly," said Grandpa, as he scooped out the pumpkin. "Speaking of traditions, shall we give our jack-o'-lantern the same face we always do?"

"Goofus!" the four kids shouted at once. That was the name they had long ago given their first goofy-looking jack-o'-lantern.

Watching her grandfather draw the lines he would soon cut, Abby asked, "Grandpa, do you think the family reunion we had last summer will become a tradition, too?"

"I hope so," said Grandpa. "It was fun, wasn't it?"

"It was the *best,*" said Abby.

Pinky and Amanda nodded in agreement.

"Maybe next summer Rex could come with us," said Pinky.

"Maybe," said Grandpa.

Abby gave Rex a funny look.

Chapter 5

The Picture

The perfect pumpkin had become the perfect jack-o'-lantern.

"Picture time!" Amanda shouted.

"It will have to wait until morning," said Grandma.

"But we *always* take our picture with Goofus," Amanda protested. "It's *tradition.* We set the camera on top of the counter, we put the timer on, we stand around Goofus—"

"Yes, yes," said Grandpa, "we know, Amanda-panda. It's tradition. But Grandma and I forgot to check the camera before we left home. There's no film in it!"

"And all the stores are closed," Grandma said. "Don't worry, we'll get film first thing in the morning and take the picture then."

"No fair," Amanda mumbled as she and Pinky and Abby went off to get ready for bed.

Rex stayed behind to look at the jack-o'-lantern one last time. It was goofy, but beautiful.

"Pretty good job, if I do say so myself," said Grandpa, resting a hand on Rex's shoulder. "But, after all, I've had years

of practice. Now, scoot, good-as-a-granddaughter. Grandma will be in in a few minutes to read to all of you."

"Okay," said Rex. She felt better than she had all day.

But then, just as she was about to go into the bathroom to brush her teeth, she heard voices from the other side of the wall.

"I know what we can do," Abby was saying. "We can get Rex to take the picture. That way she doesn't have to be in it."

"But that doesn't make sense," Pinky said. "She's always in the picture. Why shouldn't she be?"

"Because she's not part of the family," Abby answered. "That's why."

Rex waited for Pinky to say something else. But all she heard was the sound of running water and Abby giggling. "You squeezed out too much toothpaste," she said. Pinky giggled, too.

Rex lay awake for a long time that night. She listened to the trees cracking in the wind and thought how much noisier it was outside the house than inside. Over and over, she heard Abby's words: "Because she's not part of the family. That's why."

When the clock in the living room struck midnight, Rex slipped out of bed. Shivering, she tiptoed down the hall to the dining room. By the light of the moon, she could make out the jack-o'-lantern in the center of the table. It was grinning at her.

Chapter 6

A Terrible Thing

The first thing Rex heard the next morning was Grandpa calling out, "Waffles!" as he walked by the bedroom door. For the briefest moment, Rex felt excited. Grandpa's waffles were one of her favorite traditions of the weekend.

But then there came a terrible silence,

the kind that fills a house. And Rex
remembered.

"Pinky! Amanda! Abby! Get in here
at once!" she heard Grandpa shout.

Rex suddenly realized she was alone
in the room. The others must have
gotten up long ago and gone outside
to play.

"Rex!" she heard. "I think you'd better
come in here, too."

Rex tried not to think about what was going to happen.

"Well, *I* didn't do it!" Amanda was saying as Rex came into the dining room. Amanda's arms were crossed over her chest; her forehead was folded into a scowl.

"No one said you did," Grandma said. Her forehead was scowling, too, but it was more of a sad scowl than an angry one.

Grandpa, however, was mad. "Well, *someone* smashed this pumpkin, and I would like to know who did it," he said, in a voice that meant business.

"Maybe it was a burglar," Pinky suggested.

"Nonsense," said Grandpa.

"*I* know who did it," Abby said, staring right at Rex.

"*I* didn't do it," Rex said. Her cheeks were burning.

"Did, too."

"Did not. *You* did it!"

"Me?" said Abby.

"I *saw* you. And . . . and, anyway," Rex sputtered, "you're so mean, you *would* do it. You're mean and jealous!"

"Jealous?" Abby said. "*I'm* not the one who doesn't belong here!"

"Now, wait just a minute," said Grandpa.

But Rex could not wait. She burst into
tears. "I *hate* you!" she shouted. "I hate
all of you! You can take your stupid picture
without me! And without your perfect
pumpkin either! I hope you're happy!"

Rex ran back to the bedroom, slammed
the door, and threw herself on the bed.
This was the worst day of her life, she
thought, and Grandpa would never call
her his good-as-a-granddaughter again.

Chapter 7

Tradition

A little while later, Rex heard a knock on the door.

"Come in," she said in a small voice.

The door opened, and Grandma entered.

"I thought you might be getting hungry," she said to Rex.

"Not really." Rex was sitting cross-legged on the floor, next to a large drawing.

Grandma sat down on the edge of the bed next to her.

"I think we all owe you an apology, Rex," she began.

"What do you mean?" Rex asked, surprised. "I'm the one who—"

"Oh, you owe us an apology, too," Grandma went on. "What you did was wrong. But I think we understand why you did it."

Rex noticed that Abby and Pinky had come to the door. She looked down, embarrassed and ashamed.

"I'm sorry," Abby said.

"Me, too," said Pinky.

When the room fell silent, Grandma gently said, "Go on."

Abby and Pinky came in and sat down on the floor next to Rex.

"You're my best friend," Pinky said.

"I haven't been very nice."

"And you're my friend, too," said Abby, "even though I haven't been acting like it."

"You sure haven't," Rex mumbled. Then she looked right at Abby and asked, "Why?"

It was Abby's turn to look ashamed. "I guess it's because, I don't know, I had so much fun with Pinky and Amanda at the reunion last summer, I couldn't wait to see them again. I thought you'd spoil it."

"I never spoiled it before," Rex said.

"I know that," said Abby. "I was just being dumb, okay?"

"Okay."

"Friends?"

Rex tried to smile, but there was still a lot of hurt inside her.

"Me, too?" said Pinky.

"Okay," said Rex. "Friends."

"What have you been drawing?" Abby asked.

"Oh," said Rex, shifting her body so that they could see. "It's a picture of Goofus and the family. See? It's because I wrecked the real Goofus and I felt bad there would be no picture this year."

"It's good," said Pinky.

35

"Yeah," Abby agreed. "Except you
left somebody out." She picked up the
markers and began to draw. Soon there
was one more person in the picture: Rex.

"Waffles!"

Rex looked up. Grandpa was standing
in the door. Next to him was Amanda,
wearing an apron and holding a big bowl.

"Waffles for lunch, anyone?" Grandpa asked. "How about you, my good-as-a-granddaughter?"

"Okay," Rex said. She really was hungry. She hadn't known it until just that moment. "Grandpa, I . . . I'm sorry I smashed Goofus."

Grandpa looked at Rex for a moment,

then smiled. "Thank you for apologizing," he said. Then, motioning everyone to follow him down the hall, he announced, "After lunch, I have a surprise."

"A boat ride on the lake?" Amanda asked.

"Before the boat ride on the lake," said Grandpa. "I know it's hard to believe, but when I went to get film at the supermarket this morning, what do you think I found?" He pointed to the center of the dining-room table.

There sat another pumpkin. It was big and as round as the moon.

"It's perfect," said Rex.

"It is indeed," said Grandpa. "Two perfect pumpkins in one year. Now that's what I call good luck. We'll carve it right after our waffles."

"Will we call it Goofus?" Amanda asked.

"What else would we call it?" said Grandma.

"And *then* will we go for a boat ride on the lake?"

Grandpa dropped a little oil on the waffle iron, where it popped and sizzled.

"Of course we'll go for a boat ride on the lake, Amanda-panda," he said. "It's tradition!"